The Marriageable Daughter

The Marriageable Daughter

Daniel Gagnon

translated by the author

Coach House Québec Translations

First published as *La fille à marier* in 1985 by Lemeac.

Published with the assistance of the Canada Council,
the Ontario Arts Council, and the Ontario Ministry
of Culture and Communications.

Thanks to Jennifer Glossop,
and the Banff Centre School of Fine Arts, for their
assistance with this manuscript.

Text design: Nelson Adams.
Printed in Canada at
The Coach House Press, Toronto.

Canadian Cataloguing in Publication Data

Gagnon, Daniel, 1946-

[Fille à marier. English]
A marriageable daughter

(Coach House Quebec translations)
Translation of: La fille à marier.
ISBN 0-88910-376-3

I. Title.   II. Title: Fille à marier. English.   III. Series.

PS8563.A296F513 1989   C843'.54   C89-094805-4
PQ3919.2G3F513 1989

To Helen Fogwill Porter, Helen Pereira,
Phyllis Webb and Leon Rooke

á la mémoire de Gabrielle Roy

Puissions-nous, tous ensemble, troubler
la lourde sieste Canadienne.

Let us band together and shake
the heavy slumber of Canadians.

– Paul Emile Borduas

One

Dear Phyllis,

I asked my humpbacked professeur d'anglais in Sherbrooke au Québec to give me the names of young girls like me living in Canada from time immemorial, analogous to me, do me the favour of telling me, I said, the name of the young girl to whom I will write as my sister, O Phyllis, you are my dear sister in Medicine Hat, Alberta, Canada, aren't you? do you understand me well, excuse my so bad English, mister Smith mon professeur d'anglais gave me your precious name, if it will cure your pernicious anaemia, he said, and now I have my kindred soul, I am twelve and I believe it is immoral for a woman not to give herself completely to a man she loves unless she has had the poor judgment to fall in love with a man who is bad for her, then she should run a mile from him, do you, Phyllis, on the quiet, secretly read the blacklisted books in the library room of your parents, at night with a flashlight, in your pyjamas, to have the shivers, to make you shudder, to be thrilled with delight, to have a tickle in your organism? I will tell you about a boyfriend in my class, one can't help liking him, did you ever read on orgasm? it is a great mystery, I did not ask my mother, I walk on the street, I prick up my ears, the question is why deny oneself all pleasure, O Phyllis, I don't know you well, but I know you profoundly, deeply, I have no doubt I shall see him before long, do you want to hear a good deal about him? everyone is talking about orgasm, it is common gossip, we divided a cake into portions at my birthday anniversary, my parents slipped quietly away, he took my third finger, my ring finger, Phyllis, no, mister Paragraph Smith, mon professeur d'anglais, will not see this letter to sub-edit my heart, so to be a stickler for etiquette and to get on his high horse, I address this letter to you personally, do you know what an erection is, did you read about it or did you ever do see one,

Phyllis, did you? what is it exactly, I asked my big sister on the sidewalk, now if you are groaning that I'm taking all the romance out of sex and turning it into something mechanical and inhuman, you couldn't be more wrong, she said to me, so obviously there are a thousand things to say and there is not going to be time to say most of them, it is difficult to know where to begin, I am almost completely in the dark, do you like the poetess Anne Wilkinson? she writes: 'She met a lion face to face, As she went walking, Up to her lips in grass, On the wild savannah', also this: 'Then two in one the lovers lie And peel the skin of summer, With their teeth, And suck its marrow from a kiss So charged with grace, the tongue, all knowing, Holds the sap of June, Aloof from season, flowing', it is nice, Phyllis, my tongue, may sap aloft on the wild savannah two in one face to face lovers and suck their marrow from a kiss ... such is life, do you love life, Phyllis? I will marry for love, beauty is in the eye of the beholder, cold hands, warm heart, I live among cannibals at the antipodes of my feelings, in a waiting room, I walk, I am standing in the doorway, no waltz steps, to give the filthy beasts precedence, allow them to pass, go, go blotting papers, undrinkable clods, score your goal, trampling flowers down while I mark time to gather pollen, one day in burning bush go bulldozers, have sexual intercourses, to dash out hopes, to display our usual insight into human relationships and weaknesses and to question the conventional morality of the Canadian community, what do you think Phyllis about the cigarette, his name I will tell you, his name is Nicolas Champagne, he smokes secretly with me, we have a hiding place, love is not only a question of making love but love has to be done, arranged, initiated, he is the little miracle worker in my imagination, pencil of rays, did a boy ever touch you somewhere on your corpse Phyllis?

II

Oh Phyllis, do you think I should go to my gynecologist, do you have problems, if you are not overweight but just flabby or poorly proportioned, then exercise, do you wear parfum, Nicolas tells me that I smell heavenly, who could advise me how to apply makeup, what foundation is right for my skin tone, mother has several magazines that have monthly articles on makeup, do yo know what colors are flattering to you Phyllis, during your periods be sure you change your sanitary napkins and tampons often enough so there is no chance of odor build-up (said mother), smelling in the love area is not sexy, keep your fingernails and toenails clean and shampoo your hair until it squeaks, I found a book secretly in mother's room, it is called "Rapport Hite', it is about sexual pleasure, la jouissance sexuelle, one area of the body that women forget to touch is the clitoris because of its curves deep in the flesh, it remains hidden from view, I put my legs to flight, the right and wrong sides of me, reversible material in a mirror, and it is hidden from view like the princess living in a tower as if spellbound, but it is described when I touch by touch the touchstone, cursory glance, in hydroplane, babbling and purling, no I will not show my letter to mister le professeur d'anglais Smith, O Phyllis, il me semble que je te connais déjà beaucoup et par coeur, même si je ne t'ai encore jamais vue, did you understand my French words? you do not speak French in Medicine Hat of course, do you? you are too far away in that Indian country, and what do you know about me? there is much snow and lakes and we are not Americans, what is your dream? love love and love, but it is the general dream, all the people on the Planet are dreaming of love, where are the special peculiarities, do we have an attitude that is characteristic? Nicolas has his own particular way of walking, talking, unusual uncommon exceptional ordinary person, and we receive each other privately, take each other aside parental authority etc., in our family we have the same name but we are not in any way related, where are you Phyllis in the universe, my sister? it is a matter of urgency, this letter to you in the Queen's English, the wailing of a newborn infant in wanderings, roaming haphazardly, staggering vacillating wavering in vacuity in Canadian emptiness, freezing in the Pole ice from sea to sea, glorious and free, we stand on guard for thee beneath the shining skies, our home and native land, and the poor Indians, the lost Indian summer, O chère Phyllis, où es-tu, where are you, my letter will be too long, will you read it, do you think I should go to my gynecologist? I do not want to give my mother the satisfaction of going to her gynecologist, is your mother dating and going out and sleeping around a lot, what do you think about smoking pot, does it make you feel insecure and paranoid, and drugs like LSD, mushrooms, peyote and mescaline? a lot of kids trip on acid, they think it is groovy, but they do not know the dangers, chère Phyllis, I have many questions to ask of you, my kindred soul, did you ever try suicide, slashing your wrists, did you have to see a therapist, are you doing badly in school?

III

Like a stream that flows into the fleuve St-Laurent, I heave a sigh, I glance to you Phyllis in Medicine Hat, I jettison an interminable letter, to throw a bridge over a river, like a ship driven ashore by the storm! throw my letter out of the window, throw in the sponge, the die is cast, what is the score, the stakes are down, the truth is dawning on me, it is a day's journey, what is the date, what day of the week is it? I saw Nicolas the other day, he didn't see me, day by day my everyday clothes, wait till after the holidays, all the way from nowhere to nowhere, I stew in my own juice, Nicolas mon amour where is he, I swear we swore in twin

12

beds, now I am dying of natural cause, the cause of la mala-
die d'amour, it becomes apparent that I must die, it is my
only escape from a world I cannot understand! Nicolas, if
you no longer love me and do not wish me to come back to
you, will you not write and tell me so! mister professeur
d'anglais will not see my letter, because I do not want him
to see my plagiarisms neither my thoughts, my spelling
mistakes, my suicidal syntax, so Phyllis, the die is cast,
Labrador cannot be in the Rocky Mountains, what do my
friends say to me? nothing! my friend Helen started smoking when she was in sixth grade, besides pot she also
smokes cigarettes, she is not like me, I am prudish compared to her, she began having heavy sex about a year and a
half ago, just before her twelfth birthday, it was with a boy
who she really likes, they had also intercourse, I could do
that but I am afraid, I do not want to break my dream, I
psalmodize, I intone my love in my heart, I think personally that my friends who take acid and stuff like that and
have heavy sex do not really have their heads together, I do
not have friends, I am alone, alone as the north Pole, are
you alone Phyllis in Medicine Hat, what a wonderful name
for a city, charming dream of a magician who let go out of
his hat rabbits in the Prairies and also fantastic birds, and
you are in that hat, that medicare hat, Phyllis, what could
happen to you in so nice company here in Sherbrooke,
rivers wet their whistle, nothing ventured nothing gained,
so they take the plunge, jump and pole vault with coated
tongue, I skip meals, mother is anxious, I am not accom-
plishing anything, I do not want to eat, oh Nicolas où est-tu
mon amoureux, where is my Nicolas, où es-tu mon chéri,
j'ai besoin de toi, je ne peux pas vivre sans toi, mon coeur
est blessé, mon amour, Phyllis are you reading me?

Snow is snowing by inadvertence on my inappropriate world through my window, I am inaccessible, in flagrante delicto, I am a snowy neglected wife, O my lover, come to me again as once you did in snowy December, the marriageable daughter is dying with no face, a footnote to history, still in harbour, solitary, pea-size, walnut-size, like microscopic marine algae lost in the sea I shudder, I am dying out like the Labrador duck, like wild horses, giant bisons and the passenger pigeons who disappeared from the Earth, I will vanish, a girl like me cannot live, I am on the verge of extinction, my pernicious anaemia, we are a critically endangered species, Phyllis, with our fragile, delicate health and precarious happiness, anything that we do now or in the future becomes futile, in the permanent darkness of deep sea, we insinuate ourselves into small crevices between rocks, we tend to be secretive, living on hard bottoms where little sun penetrates, O the light! Phyllis, we feed on small particles of light, we extend arms into the water and catch suspended particles, but I am tired out, what medicine would act to exhume me from the buried continent, Phyllis, do you have a remedy in your beautiful hat for me, wreathed with mist, a fountain of wisdom to save me from violence, discord and confusion, from pride and arrogance, and from every evil way, a prayer to give me back my lover Nicolas, to defend our love and fashion us into one united person, Nicolas and me, brought hither out of many kindreds and tongues, to deliver us from evil, and grant us an entrance into the land of light and joy, in the fellowhship of the saints, in the eternal and everlasting glory, oh I have a terrible headache, I will let my passport expire, I am losing the thread, the ship is in distress, the plane is crashing to the ground, my brain is crippled with rheumatism, many questions will not be answered.

V

My dear partridge Phyllis, why am I writing to you in the
Prairies, so far from me in Canada, perhaps it is because I
do not know you at all and it is easier for me to talk, I cannot
talk to my girlfriends à l'école Ste-Marguerite de Sherbrooke, neither to my mother or my older sister, they do
not know me, I do not know these strangers, they do not see
I am in danger, jeopardized perilously, I am choking on a
fishbone at the table and nobody helps me, I am parched
with thirst and my family is a desert, si je t'écrivais en
français, tu ne comprendrais rien et eux ils connaîtraient
tous mes secrets, oh Phyllis, chère amie, I know you understand me, my kindred soul, my unknown sister neverthe-
less, in spite of everything, in spite of my clumsiness,
despite my awkwardness, even though you are in another
part of the world, there is no distance, no language, no time
between us, you could be my grandmother or my daughter, I can expose my heart, confide my secrets to you, my
nearest relation, my blood transfusion, O I love you
Phyllis, my good spirit, I have lost power of speech, only
you, Phyllis, my sister, can hear me and understand,
because you do not exist, I can talk to you my dear ghost,
my double in a magician's hat far away in the Far West,
where I like to hear the fortune-teller making up a new love
story, I am hypnotized by the formidable hat, the holy hat
coming down from heaven, lighting upon the Canadians,
teaching them, leading them into all truth, giving them the
bold zeal to preach the Medicine Hat unto all provinces,
whereby we have been brought out of darkness and error
into the clear light and true knowledge of thee, where we
are with angels, O Phyllis my pure angel, do not listen to
my blasphemies, throw my letter out of the window, I hope
I will never send you this string of absurdities, I write only
for myself in the obscure hell of my dead love in the family
vault, my parents will outlive me and nobody will ever

know, personne ne connaîtra jamais ma peine ni mon cha-
grin, O Phyllis, close your eyes and go to bed, let us sleep
side by side and alongside our pernicious anaemia, it is late
and everything is okay now, you sleep and dream while I
hold myself here on my backside with clenched hands,
R.I.P., requies in pace, forgive me.

VI

If my mother could see this English letter I am writing to
you now, Phyllis, she would be very angry, she would
smack my face or cry, ask me if I love her, I would not
answer, I would want only to die because I love her so
much in the meantime I do not love her at all, I am a traitor,
Mother, go away, I cannot love you, let me alone, I will kill
myself, I do not have the right to live anymore, I will take
poison or slash my wrists, yes, I will enter a state of pro-
longed sleep, my temperature will drop close to the freezing point, I will migrate, mind barren of ideas, harassed by
warble and nostril flies that bore into my flesh, I will reach
the North Pole to dress the bride, to decorate the marriageable daughter, to embellish the paralytic anaemic girl
metamorphosed into an ice cube on Ellesmere Island, then
the bulls having already arrived and established territories and collected harems of cows, will not see me in the
Eastern Townships, the daughter will not begin to mate at
the age of twelve to let her dress trail in the dust, she will
not make a tragedy out of her death, mother was an adoles-
cent mother, Phyllis, and my English grandmother took
care of me when mother and I came home from the hospital, after, because of the hostility between my mother and
my grandmother, I was placed in foster care, after, I went
back with my French mother, here in Sherbrooke au
Québec, where I am writing to you, O excuse my irrelevan-
cies, I am turning the knife in the wound, my unquenched
soul in these unquiet times, there are 615 streets in Sher-

brooke and where are you Nicolas? Nicolas, où es-tu mon amour? O Phyllis, will you act as go-between in our love affair? I owe you more than I can repay, I will pray for you in the melting, in the thawing of the snow.

VII

Like a fossil, I am not especially pretty, I must adapt myself to a short loving season, a severe, cold treeless, arctic affection, I am a tundra region, I am covered with bogs, I am a spongy mat of decayed lichens and grasses in the desert of love, under this Arctic Cathedral hoar frost is our mantle, my skin is mottled from the cold, where am I, where are we, Phyllis, are we with hominids, the Ramapithecus, the monkey, the Australopithecus robustus africanus, the Neanderthals, millions of years ago? your father is an Homo erectus and, believe it or not, your mother is an Homo erectus too, Homo erectus learned the use of fire, with fire they warmed themselves, lighted the darkness to ward off real and imagined terrors, O Phyllis, I have no fire in the night, me, Homo (Femina) sapiens, I do not see, do you see something in the twentieth century's emptiness? they cook and tenderize their meat, but they have a heart of stone, for countless millennia nothing happened, ah, pauvre amie, me voilà encore en train de broyer du noir, pardonne-moi ma chérie, mon âme soeur, pense à moi, O forgive me, my dear kindred sister.

VIII

The marriageable daughter would wear long filigree earrings attached to each of her ear lobes, and be beautiful, why not swing, people would say to her, why not fool around with boys, take the pill, you will not have to worry about getting pregnant, sex is nothing but fun, they would say again to her, what is that senseless extravagant idea of marriage? the marriageable daughter would not answer, she would pound those words to a jelly, a hash for the masses, the masochistic majority slaughtered by the butchers, the politicians and the companys' presidents steaming without lights and masked, disguising their smell, Phyllis, will you come from Medicine Hat to my marriage with long beautiful legs and a nice sunhat in a wagon, prince consort in a tail coat, a hunk of bread for a picnic lunch, our corsets will lace up at the side, labyrinthine and languorous we will have the word love on the tips of our tongues, we will unseal our eyes and see the sun rise, vivified, singing songs and contemplating the flight of birds, come, the lamp is fading, my wick is flickering, I died yesterday, come, I was desperately in love with Nicolas, O Nicolas, where are you, the horse lives forty-five years, the bear twenty-five years, dogs and cats fifteen years, and me, twelve years in captivity, my bones are not ossified yet, I grew at a fetal rate and I reached maturity too fast, in a poor soil I suffer from love's senility, my heart is very old, it lived far more intensely than an elephant's heart which lives seventy years or than my mother's heart which does not beat the same number of times in shopping centres, in front of television or at the telephone.

IX

There is a baby growing inside my body Phyllis, I do not believe it, maybe it is only a tumor or I am getting a little fat, I cannot believe that there is another human being inside me, O Nicolas! ce serait notre fils ou notre fille, notre enfant, our child! if it is really a baby, I will keep him and raise him, I will drop out of school and stay home, I reject abortion, mother will help me, he will be my main reason for living, my mother does not want to speak to me, she acts sullen, but the baby will be very cute and she will love her little grandson, if not I will move out of the potato family, the mustard family, but perhaps there is no baby, perhaps my developing fruit has already atrophied, wizened, gone amuck. I am a flower split open to show her fleshy receptacle, her interior ovary, her branches with dry leaves, her stamens and pistils, Phyllis, I am like lilies grown for ornamental purposes, but in the species of lilies who yield drugs and have poisonous properties, I have three times as much as I need and I swim against the stream, the poison works against me, I absorb it and become asexual and sterile, I do not eat anymore, Phyllis, you are reading my testimony, I bequeath my petals, my dried tears, my ovules, my corolla, my wedding dress to you, my kindred flower, I will be incorporated into the organic world and become compost and the molecules of dead leaves and dung, ding dong the bells, I will move along chains of electrons to other lives, I will be a tomato plant or a pea, not a violated flower, I do not want to be nice and cute, my ice-cube heart is blooming in thousands of crystallized stars, you would think the marriageable daughter was asleep at the crossroads but instead she is crying in the north wind from the rooftop of the planet.

X

I do not ask my mother if she is happy, she is too busy keeping the house going, the potato family, she has to go shopping, she has to answer the telephone, cook apples and make apple pies, see the psychiatrist, the gynecologist, I could not tell her I got my period in July, I started menstruating when I was ten years old, I had my own napkins, she told me that babies grow in the stomach, I thought the baby would come out my anus not my vagina, our bodies are so small, how could they expand enough? can the blind lead the blind? shall they not both fall into the ditch? the disciple is not above his master, but everyone that is perfect shall be as his master, and why beholdest thou the beam that is in thy brother's eyes, but perceivest not the beam that is thine own eye, thou hypocrite, cast out first the beam, school is a game, you have to get the marks to stay there, I will drop that whole bag, it is not my scene anymore, Mister Smith mon professeur d'anglais lives for teaching, he does not know what to do at thirty-seven, he is too old, I told him about my developing fruit, his fruit, our baby in my body, it was an accident of course, because my lover is Nicolas, only Nicolas, never with Nicolas have I done those things, but that evening at home, mon professeur was there with me, he is not my lover, I do not know what happened.

<hr>

XI

Perhaps mon professeur could hold my hand and come with a gift for the baby, play baseball with my little brother and show me his wisdom teeth as gold as gold in his sacristan mouth, he wants to help me, to sacrifice himself for me, it makes his heart bleed, he orders me to eat, I will not anymore, he will not see this English letter either, he is sitting in the orchestra stalls, I say to him, you put a satellite in orbit, if it should come to the headmaster's ears you can imagine how angry he will be, I have a high opinion of you, mister Paragraph, but I am on a downward path, the rudder braces are broken, go, mister, I will take a three-room flat, one for me, one for Phyllis and one for my baby, your fingers, mister professor, are drumming on the tablecloth, the smoke makes my eyes sting, go now, I have to speak to Phyllis rabbiting in Medicine Hat with her many thoughts, yes Phyllis, mon professeur d'anglais fell in love with me, he is handsome, kind, gentle, the only person I could talk to, and now unless he can stop himself he is going to ruin his marriage, he wants to quit his job, stay home and treasure the baby and me, but I am in love with Nicolas, I say this to him, he is feeling a rush of emotion, he blushes deeply and can hardly talk, he feels so overwhelmed, it is totally unexpected, don't you think, Phyllis? he fantasizes more and more about me, he even thinks about me while he is making love with his wife, I will not talk with him about diapers, sleep schedules and feeding problems, because there is no more baby in me.

XII

I will not do exercises to enlarge my breasts and I will not start wearing a bra, the weight of my breasts does not require support, because I have no breasts and I will never have, mother has had a mastectomy and a big scar remains, I saw it, over her heart, I will not accent my eyes with shadow, liner, coats of mascara, I will not camouflage my under-eye circles, I will not have any reconstructed nipples because I will not live, Phyllis, I am not afraid of cancer, cancer is a benediction, all those humans who live too long with stone hearts like old machines, keeping their skin clean, moist, with night creams, baby oils, massages, petroleum jelly, lotions etc., I do not gently wash away those dead cells that can clog my pores and cause skin problems, I cultivate my skin problems, I am proud of them, of my spotty, pimply face, I am always ready to show the squint in my left eye and to thank God that my clothes are falling to pieces, I feel like a wreck, like a wet rag, I shut the door of my room and keep it on the latch, my short life is a novel full of tedious passages, a protracted winter, time seems to drag, I am getting bored, O Phyllis, you do not know the sadness of my life, no joy, no delight, no gladness, I am under the spell of Cinderella, tit for tat, a ship dragging its anchor.

XIII

There is nothing that we should be particularly proud of in the decadent mentality of the twentieth century, like kings and dictators, tsars, emperors and queens, I have heard many rich people have sex with young girls like me, they say Joseph Stalin visited schools in Russia to kidnap young girls and keep them imprisoned to nourish his mad love, his sexual urge and his degenerate passion for us, little girls, like my professeur d'anglais mister Paragraph, but he is not a maniac, he loves the firmness of my flesh, my idealism, the grandeur and the nobility of my young soul, my newness, the hope I represent, and I do not love him, I love Nicolas and I want to die, but life seems to last forever, I pluck my eyebrows, no need to go on commenting, my sleep is disturbed, I have no appetite, life is a persistent nightmare for me, in this century people do not really know anymore what is good or bad, they can hurt and they do not know, they do not want to know they are hurting, with their stony hearts, sex for many of my friends, Phyllis, is simply a pleasure thing, we are four-footed beasts in a film, they have sold their souls to the devil, to a disillusioned mind, an older generation wants to steal the freshness, the innovativeness, the excitement that we can bring to lovemaking, if they only could make that hour last forever as in the Heaven with the Father Eternal, but this hour is a part of the underworld, there is no love and where there is not love there is hell, O Phyllis, I have been cooped up each day of my twelve years, I smell stuffy, do not read me anymore, throw my letter out of the window, America is moving with the times and is heading for disaster, the ship goes down with all hands, leucorrhoea and flooding, the spinal cord is attacked, the corn-husking party is ending while ship pilots shrug their shoulders and girls pin up their hair, looking for a needle in a haystack to get out of a ticklish situation, spick and span despite their unhappiness, nobody is able to drive away pain and sickness of soul and body, I am soured by misfortune and failings, I am walking in the desert, Phyllis, at one with the uncertainty of human life, the sorrows, errors and difficulties of the world, I am lying in great weakness of body, these days are without end, O I want to die, my professeur d'anglais is not responsible, he is sure I have found pleasure, I am so depressed, moody and lost in my thoughts, he has not been involved with me, I must tell you frankly, he has contributed to my life only by his English lessons, Phyllis, he does not even exist, no, there is no mister Paragraph professeur d'anglais or anybody with a name like that, I do not even exist myself, only you, my dear friend, my kindred soul, my angel, only you, Phyllis, exist, with Nicolas, only you two.

XIV

Bending over the cradle, mortally wounded by the firing squad, I return home a stillborn child, I am standing in a corner by myself, while they whisper among themselves, I am resigned to it, I lay up the ship, I leave the world in the lurch, I shelve the project, I quit, scraping the bottom of the barrel, no love, Phyllis, to strike at the root of the evil will be necessary, one day atomic bombs will speak in the cities to redeem mankind, I am not a radar operator, I will not enlist supporters, mother spins long yarns, tells some fine stories, whatever is she saying? it is just tittle-tattle, the folly and vanity of those things with which most people occupy their lives, they don't want the truth, O Phyllis, it is dreadful, they feel no awe, they shun romance, they seek dusty answers and useless wealth, their dystrophy rolls them up into a ball, they are tadpoles from head to foot, grey-headed old men and women dying intestate like terriers whisking their tails in the zoological gardens, O, I am in a constant melancholy, discontent, I want to sink into a tranquil sleep, goodbye my friend, going, going, gone! I make my way silent and unknown, O Nicolas, my dear love, my sweetheart, come, where are you? I will go with you into another world where you are now my darling, after your death of last Monday I promised myself to walk hand in hand with you into the cosmos, along the alley of the Milky Way we will find happiness together as we found it here in the city, we will marry again, we will give each other more and more, we have not ceased to love each other, Nicolas, mon amoureux chéri, tu n'es pas mort, tu ne seras jamais mort pour moi, tu vivras toujours, éternellement! my love, you are not dead, you will never die, you will live eternally, I am not happy, Nicolas, are you? are you content without me in some Paradise or purgatory, I live here among mountains of snow and rivers of ice, did you enter gorgeous temples where we could marry again dressed in rich robes? O I want to jump the rails, to leave the putrefactive fermentation, to join you in death, my love, O mon amoureux chéri, Nicolas, tends-moi les mains, viens me chercher, come take me with you my darling! with blinking eyes we will pitch a tent for ourselves in the vault of heaven.

Two

XV

I feel a lot older than my twelve years, we suffer, Phyllis, don't we? among mortals, we have not attained our desire, and disenchantment is heavy upon us, dances, parties, feasts, revels are nothing without love, O pure and kind Phyllis, we lay up treasures upon earth which rust corrupts and which thieves break through and steal, but there is nothing to steal because I have nothing, far in the north in an ice cube I live alone, immutable, will I stand resuscitated with Nicolas in everlasting youth and bloom? how miserable you and I are here, Phyllis, O Nicolas, we could sit together, perhaps you could hold my hand and I could hold yours, we could walk in the 615 streets of Sherbrooke, arm in arm, O Phyllis, I see him, he walks with me, he is not dead, he kisses my mouth, we embrace, we do not talk, in awe we listen to the sound of our hearts in our veins, in our rib cages, the gracious moon is emerging from the clouds, from her prison and her fastenings, in the armour of righteousness, ours sincerely, giving us her regards, riding bareback in the sky over Hudson Bay, North Ontario, Manitoba and Saskatchewan to rejoin the Medicine Hat, the Magician Hat in the Prairies where she comes from, the moon is eternal and spiritual, not temporal and material, she strolls serene in the heavens, keeping a discreet watch on frail mortals, redeeming fallen humanity, soothing the marriageable daughter's afflictions and tumults and inducing in her the fruits of love by means of gaiety, prosperity and twenty-eight-day periods of glory, O the moon, Nicolas, we will strike off for the moon, we will mount this golden horse and travel together in the cosmos, we will plough through the high solar winds and cross rains of meteorites in the armour de l'amour, we will arise from death every blessed day without sunglasses, what joy, what gladness! our flesh radiant with this triumph over suffering and deprivations, this victory reflected in our visage and our conduct, we will listen in mute astonishment, silent as the grave, to the sound of eternity.

XVI

They experiment with the 'distressed' look in makeup, they do not know what distress is in my class, they go to the disco almost every night, burn incense in their bedrooms, look older than they are, wash their faces with soap and water twice a day, care, really care about their skin, how it looks, how it feels, they live like cattle, they give me a wry smile as though I were a piece of wreckage, my stockings are wrinkled, they wring their hands in despair, they are like wine that has lost its sparkle, with their unfeeling hearts they would consent to my execution on the charge of blasphemy and punish me by stoning, O Phyllis, the tortures and agony I endure are horrible enough, but the cruelest torments and my deepest anguish are not physical pains, my sufferings are moral, I am isolated, deserted, with no intimate companions, where are my friends, my brothers and my sisters? O Phyllis, why do they reject me? perhaps the marriageable daughter should commit suicide, choking with sobs in this self-sufficient America that reeks of crime? there are limits to the conditions human beings can tolerate, sex is nothing but fun, war is nothing but fun in the Earthly Paradise, the lights have fused, it is drizzling now, the cheese is crawling with maggots, there has been a foul-up in the foundations of modern society, O Phyllis, excuse me, forgive me, throw my letter out of the window, I am at the window, send me a medicine from the magic hat, I am wounded, I am falling to my death.

28

Large eyes, long antennae, membranous wings, slender body, the damsel fly died in a fatal embrace, a firefly had seized and was feeding on her, I flew toward him, giving my damsel fly signal again and again, the exchange led to an affinity between us, harmonious arrangement, O Phyllis, the marriageable daughter has been captured, she fell prey to temptation, a male firefly (O, he is so beautiful, so luminescent!) preys on me, if he is an enemy I love my enemy, oh Nicolas reviens, j'irai te rejoindre dans l'au-delà, pourquoi ne me poursuis-tu plus? why did you cease to pursue me, I am haunted by you, hear my courtship song, I rub the femur of my third pair of legs, listen to the passionate hum caused by my fluttering wings and my vibrating membranes, I take my pulse rushing frantically around, my heart misses a beat, I suffer from palpitations, let us fly away together, ah! the damsel fly is no longer a damsel, she has torn her wings, she is now a termite going forth at night among enormous foraging armies to gather humus, leaf litter and lichen.

XVIII

Phyllis, is your father one of those cowboys and capitalists who go after the bulls in the Prairies with a firm grasp on the rope around the beast's neck? oh Sherbrooke, you know, is not a shining city rising from the sea! making a mountain out of a molehill, my mother is not rich, she was an esthetician, if you have a father, is he rich, does he own department stores, airlines, hotels, insurance companies, television networks, breweries and distilleries, railways, banks, gold mines, coal pits and oil wells? does he emply bodyguards and not accept telephone calls, do you have a villa in Nassau or a castle above the Rhine? Phyllis, can you talk to the magician and ask him to find in his medicine hat a medal of Saint-Christophe for the marriageable daughter, so I can travel to Nicolas my love, I do not want a pair of shoes nor a new dress in purple and fine linen, O Phyllis, I will drag you down with me, do not listen to me, wrap me in a clean linen cloth, lay me in my own tomb and roll a great stone to the door of the sepulchre without hesitating, I am a weak anaemic creature, full of sores and rheumatism, but I know the reality and the sincerity of Nicolas's love, he is invisible but his nature is made known to me by his light waves.

XIX

I am poorly adapted to the season because I flowered prematurely, I have been exposed to love and now, at twelve, already in my menopause, feet close together, I live in continuous darkness, my internal and biological clock is broken, the one hotspot in which I could flower again is hell, there I could surely find my polygamous father, whom I poisoned with arsenic in his soup, dead and gone, when the police inspector came I put on a suitable expression, a poker-face, the funeral will be private, said my mother, she did not want to see all of my late father's mistresses, your father, she said, has escaped uninjured and unhurt, one must choose the lesser of two evils, there is no harm in that, he has no cause to regret his life, I will not speak ill of him, he packed his trunk as artfully as a cartload of monkeys, and abandoned us, I was unlucky, a miserable five-cent piece in my purse, où irons-nous, Jeanne? my mother asked me (although I hate her I will help her), it is the worldweariness, I said to mother, just take a sick leave, but I have no more job, she said, I retorted: your job, it is me, mother, and very soon I shall go like father, oh my legs are giving way beneath me, Phyllis, it is World War Three, I am tilting at windmills like Don Quixote, I am a chatterbox and a windbag, do not listen to me, forgive me, O my darling in your fabulous hat, holy, holy, holy, Lord Hat Almightly, which was, and is, and is to come.

<hr>

XX

My granulated grandmother was born in 1919 in Québec City of English parentage, educated at Bishop's University and McGill, she travels, she writes English letters, she talks, talks and talks, her words and her journeys are her collected poems, her anthology, her dead works, she searches her identity but she thinks she has none, and I think she does not exist, I have no grandmother, I love her very much, Phyllis, but I do not have ancestors, I am an orphan, I only have you, Phyllis, in the world, nobody else, sometimes I speak to her apparition, I converse with the phantom of my grandmother, pure wheaten flour, her head filled with romantic ideas, I am not romatic, I hate romanticism, she writes letters, I have never seen her, she is always on conducted tours around the world, not far from here in a mental hospital, she wrote me in a recent letter: 'Dear Jeanne, you will be surprised to get the hundredth letter from me away off here – I have been taking quite a journey the last two months – have been out to the Rocky Mountains and Colorado – 2,000 miles (seems to me I sent you a missive six weeks ago from Denver) – I got along very well until three weeks ago when I was taken sick and disabled, and hauled in here in Medicine Hat for repairs, have been here ever since – am fixed comfortable – still somewhat under the weather (but have no doubt I shall be well as usual for me before long) – shall stay here probably two or three weeks longer, and then back east to Québec – Jeanne, this is a wonderful country out here, and no one knows how big it is until he launches out in the midst of it – but there are plenty of hard-up fellows, many young men, some old chaps, some boys of fifteen or sixteen – I meet them everywhere, especially at the railway stoppings, out of money and trying to get home – but the general run of all these western places, city and country, is very prosperous, on the rush, plenty of people, plenty to eat, and apparently plenty of money, in Medicine Hat – found a soldier here who had known my father in the War fifteen years ago – was married and running the hotel here – I had hard work to get away from him – he wanted me to stay all winter – the picture at the beginning of this letter is the bridge over the Rivière Saskatchewan – I often go down to the river, or across this bridge – it is one of my favourite sights – I met there a young girl like you – Well, Jeanne, dear girl, I guess I have written enough – how are you getting along? I often think of you and no doubt you often do of me – God bless you, my darling friend, and however it goes you must keep a good heart – for I do – so long – from your old granulated grandma.'

XXI

I was still doubtful about speaking to mon professeur d'anglais when he gave me a lift downtown, a man is judged by his actions, he told me, when I showed him the scars on my thighs made with a branding iron by my father, I felt sleepy, mon professeur wanted very much to touch my flesh wound, he was eaten up with compassion, mon professeur said that the love of our neighbour is the outward test by which you may know the reality and sincerity of your inward love, do not turn the knife in the wound, you put your finger on the source of the trouble, I said, give me a sign revealing your true person and mission, mister professeur, you are hardened against accepting the way in which my expectations are fulfilled in Nicolas, particularly in his beauty as an outcast and neglected pauper, man does not live by bread only, I need him, all you professeurs, fathers and old men are trying to survive, you have lost love, you have closed your eyes and blinded your hearts to the light, and I will not have any child by you, you are enough of a child, life is not just a rat race, no, you will not find me or anybody else, no soul, you will incur your own displeasure by turning over each girl like pages of a love magazine, each one has only one love, did your love slip quietly away during your youth? aren't you able to recapture it? not with me, my father, you tried in the name of the ties that bind me to the family, you won't catch me doing that again, because now you are dead and killed by my rat poison in your Bluebeard soup, you had your chance, I will not keep the child, father's or professeur's child, I do not mind, I will not need an abortion because there is no child in me, no bird in the bush, no nest, just pourousness, you are the little shrimps, the squirts, and in addition I am dying, I will no longer exist so there will be no problem at all, I am my own child, no, I am a woman, Nicolas made me a real woman, he passed away in my arms, no longer subject to the decay of his physical body or to the bondage of time over his heart and his love, but he is not dead, it is me who is dead, one dead and two injured: me, him, and the baby, I will lie down in white naphthalene in balls, in an oil slick, in a lava flow, in a nebula, protecting my love from the changes of time, waiting for resurrection. O Phyllis, forgive my eager hopes, I am flying blind, sad as February showers and stunted trees, I shall soon be finished, I will commit suicide in my bath, you will never see this letter, ask my grandmother on the bridge over the Saskatchewan River about me, no news is good news, O my white water lily, give her a kiss for me if you see her, don't tell her who I am now, she knows already how revolting, what an awful and frightful object I am.

XXII

I have been exposed to radioactivity, all my cells are damaged and my mechanism defective, I cannot repair myself, I cannot restore the original structure, I will never recover my breath, my courage, my consciousness, I am destroyed by the heat of passion, I am now only this potato jacket who is writing to you, Phyllis, attention à toi mon âme soeur, look out, like a flea or a louse I might transmit an infection to you, I transmit plague or typhus, do not read my letter, my sweetheart, where would you find a vaccine? would you like to come with me to an ice cube at the North Pole, or into a lava flow, or a nebula, waiting for the whole realm of creation, animate and inanimate, when the curse of suffering and corruption brought into this world by the Fall of Eve will be no more and when girls will regain their true destiny of love? O come, Phyllis, the result would surpass our hopes, exceed our desires, it would be the glorious transfiguration in the cosmos, we would get out of the smallpox, the house does not suit us, would you like to quit on All Saints Day? knot your shoelaces, andante, we will eat the heavenly manna and drink the miraculous water, we will walk among the vigorous plants in the Garden of Eden, among the shrubs and the trees, the weeping willows, the violas, the hollyhocks, the magnolias, the aquilegia, on an Arabian camel, we will eat flowers, poisons and drugs, belladonna and opium, we will swallow their milky latex, God's sperm, at sundown in pyjamas, blue with a white stripe, like mares' tails in the sky we will run in the fields with the billion microscopic droplets of the evening dew, and we will drop down and lie there with dream-bright faces for eternity.

XXIII

Another letter of grandmother: 'Dear Jeanne, well, here I am launched on my seventy-third year. We had our birth anniversary spree last evening. About forty people – choice friends mostly – twelve or so women. We had a capital good supper – chicken soup, salmon, raost lamb, etc. etc., I had been under a horrible spell from five to six, but Warry got me dressed (like carrying down a great log) and Traubel had all ready for me a big goblet of first-rate champagne – I swigged it off at once. I certainly welcomed them all forthwith and at once felt if I was to expire I would not expire without a desperate struggle. Must have taken near two bottles of champagne that evening ... Nothing very new or different – bad enough – the fiendish indigestion block continued – heavy torpor increasing – the burial house in Medicine Hat well toward finished – I paid the constructor $5,000 last week –. I wish to collect the remains of my parents and two or three other near relations and shall doubtless do so – I have two deceased children (young man and woman – illegitimate of course) that I much desired to bury here with me, would you come, Jeanne?'

'P.S.: Jeanne, read this (it's me!) my star-given temperament this month): Aquarius, the commitment-shy Uranus girl is slow to love. Your sign needs to explore – so many glories in the world – and you jealously guard your freedom, preferring to marry excitingly and late. It makes you the most dreamily romantic of all signs (!!). Aquarius is also a critical sign, subjecting lovers to the closest scrutiny, and you've a somewhat changeable heart, Uranus-given curiosity means you prefer a heady, fast-moving parade of partners to a lackluster long-term affair, you are a sexy snugglebug some of the time but need frequent retreats into solitude to stay emotionally fresh (!). Adieu, ma petite Jeanne, ta grand-mère qui t'embrasse.'

XXIV

Even if we were happy at the time of our birth, Phyllis, we will be happy again only at the time of our death, O death is beautiful, my kindred sister! why shouldn't we stay with her, the Lady Death, Madame la Mort? why shouldn't we be citizens of her kingdom? the beauty we had planned sleeps in her forever, only a few black flowers in memory will be left by us for many centuries on this Earth, a few pieces of caramelized bones, without rhyme or reason, hominid fossils a thousand years old, quelle importance alors de partir ou de rester maintenant? descending from the train, two children, you and me, arm in arm, see a vast playground, an immense circus for sale, the director is in a generous mood and in a poetic vein, he sells us all on credit, he asks us if we are getting married, I say I am the marriageable daughter with my kindred soul Phyllis Dalton, and my grandmother is singing behind us, we want to marry, where is Nicolas? we want to get married, all three of us, me Jeanne, Phyllis and Nicolas, but Nicolas is not there, he is a little horse on the carousel, he is a prisoner of the circus charm, he cannot run away, he is turning in euphoria for all eternity, O Phyllis, then I cry, cry, and I ask the director for a ride on the little horse Nicolas, go, go, he says, the carousel is yours, my young girls, I sold it to you, but do not, please, break the spell, I love him, I say, well, says the circus director, ask the village blacksmith to forge golden horseshoes for you and your friend, so you will be able to get on the merry-go-round, watch out for wild beasts, and it will be an incredible and delightful story! can we invite my grandmother, she is so alone, she would like to escape from prison, dust and corruption, to survive her illness and come to Death with us? O Phyllis, what epitaph will express the warmth of our friendship and the light that showered upon us in the heat of our youth, exact fit of a screw in the hell where everyday passions are boiling in continuous apoplectic stroke, I will write a note for mother telling her that thieves have stripped the house and that I have been kidnapped from the kitchen by demons in tail coats and that the marriageable daughter has found her charming prince et son royaume infiniment chaleureux, you surely do not know, mother, how cold it is, in spite of everything, in the ice cube, demons are so cold that they are hot, the tents are stretched and the igloos are shaped, it is snowing in hell, believe it or not, il neige de la neige, black ice, glaze on roads, Satan, he is not a beauty, anybody will tell you that, but he is not dictatorial, stark naked like a glow worm, why does he live on, buried alive in an iceberg? I don't know, I got lost in the snowy plains all night (or all day, it is the same) and there were wolves and polar bears, but Phyllis, you came to me on a draught horse which was Nicolas running away from the circus world, and I could not climb it, his hands could not reach me, O mother, forgive me.

XXV

However much I may have abused your goodness, mother, however far I may have searched for you, like bones that are joined together in a dancing skeleton, my joy rattles and clinks in the darkness for the rest of my days, hiding my face among the steppes of the North Pole, I live with the demons and the unfair beasts, O mother, you would like to see me at this moment, you would give me another chance, you would be so gentle and companionable and tender, but I am dead in the passageway and I like it like that, I have friends, grandmother, and Phyllis and Nicolas my love, we sit on the hot snow dunes, staring at the sky where we will never go, great wings of devils whirl above us thick as gnats behind our eyelids, the wind in a passing whim whispers and whips, telling fairytales, imagine me, mother, wearing my unfashionable dress, silhouetted against the light background, making the sign of the cross and inviting demons to my wedding with Father Christmas, the wicked fairy Carabossa, Puss-in-Boots, the Sleeping Beauty, the Beauty and the Beast and Tom Thumb, do you see the light burning, the shadows that hop about, the corpses on fire, the river of blood overflowing its banks? c'est l'enfer, I fill my lungs with the smell of the crematorium, the tattoo marks of the demons, the peacocks on their biceps, the eagles, the snakes on their naked bodies, they mount and ride astride each other in libidinous and lustful jousts and tilts, there are Hitler and Judas, Khadafy and Richard Nixon, and my own father crying out for vengeance, grinding his teeth, as it is written, the people sit down to eat and drink, and rise up to play, and commit fornication, the end of the world has arrived, there is no way to escape from the serpents and crocodiles, no firemen in the eternal fire, only passion, lions, ana-condas, hyenas and tigers, among them I dream of love's ecstasies and inspired utterances, no liars or hypocrites here, no fake or fair promises, I live with equanimity, O for-give me, mother, where else can I go except hell, the basis of my faith and hope, but, O mother, hell does not exist, hell is on Earth with you, but you will never know because I am writing this letter in english and you do not understand english, and I am writing to Phyllis Dalton in Medicine Hat, Alberta, Canada, and you do not know her, neither do I, and I will not send this letter, I will eat it after I finish and spew it up and vomit, I still live on Earth, mother, in Sherbrooke, Montréal, Trois-Rivières, Rouyn, Sept-Iles, Toronto, on the street like a junkie, I sleep in tourist rooms, cars and hotels, boats and streets, dancing in night clubs, drinking poisons, eating mushrooms and pricking myself, you will not see this letter, nor me, ever again, I will not phone, my child will not live, O maman chérie! je suis abandonnée et perdue, pardonne-moi, forgive me, please do.

'Ma chère petite Jeanne, dear comrade, you must be assured that my heart is much with you and with my other dear friends, your associates – and, my dear, I wish you to excuse me to your father, should you see him – how I should like to see him and have a good heart's time with him, and a mild orgy, just for a basis, you know, for talk and interchanges of reminiscences and the play of the quiet lambent electricity of real friendship – O Jeanne, as my pen glides along, writing these thoughts, I feel as if I could not delay coming right off and seeing you all, you and Nicolas, and everybody – I want to be within hand's reach of you, and hear your voices, even if only for one evening, I still live here in Medicine Hat, I am writing this in Michael's Motel, more often than not I go for a walk down the river, O the sad scenes of this world – scenes of death, anguish, friendlessness, hungering and thirsting young hearts, for some loving presence – such noble young girls as some of these wounded are – such endurance, such native decorum, such candor – Best love to your father – Je t'embrasse tendrement, ma petite Jeanne adorée, ta grand-mère qui s'ennuie. Your granulated grandmother. P.S.: I feel well and hearty enough, and was never better, but my feelings are kept in painful condition a great part of the time, things get worse and worse, I get almost frightened at the world, I could not keep the tears out of my eyes last Friday night, it was a dreadful night – pretty dark, the wind gusty, and the rain fell in torrents, one poor girl – she seemed to be quite young, je n'ai pu m'empêcher de penser à toi, my darling, oh ça me fait pleurer – she was quite small (I looked at her body afterwards), she groaned some as the stretcher bearers were carrying her along, they set down the stretcher and examined her, and the poor girl was dead (suicide), they took her into the ambulance, and a doctor came immediately, but it was all of no use, the worst of it is, too, that she is entirely unknown – there was nothing on her clothes, or anyone with her to identify her, she is altogether unknown, Jeanne darling, it is enough to rack one's heart such things, very likely her folks will never know in the world what has become of her, poor, poor child, for she appeared as though she could be but twelve ...'

XXVII

O Phyllis, my kindred soul, tell me it is not you the poor girl who dived at twelve into the Rivière Saskatchewan! tell me it is not you! maybe it is me, do you think? how could it be me, Medicine Hat is too far from Sherbrooke au Québec, unless I had been kidnapped and raped in a train or a plane and dropped in the Hat, O how hopelessly we stand under the condemnation of this world! we are sanitary napkins that are tossed on the landscape, our beings have been vandalized in superannuated schools and by a superfluity of words, the people who think themselves important in this world may well find that, in the Kingdom of Hell, their place of privilege will be taken by others, they never burnt so they will never burn, no lukewarm people in the underworld, no tepid love in the inferno, l'enfer brûle, no self-centred or self-regarding, all of them bought their heaven at a discount, O Phyllis, we resist all forms of weakness and baseness when we plunge into the river, after our one true only love the pure passion and imagination of our heart grows fully and infinitely, let us commit suicide together, wait for me, my kindred friend, and alas! I am sure Nicolas is in heaven and I will never be able to find him, Phyllis, to join my love! what could I do, he died because his parents killed him to give one more angel to the church, yes, they robbed me of him, my only treasure, mon amour, toute ma vie, ils me l'ont dérobé, he was beautiful, he loved me and he would have come with us to eternity, but his parents sacrificed him to pay their own passage to heaven, yes

Phyllis, the moon is on the wane, the marriageable daughter will not marry, she cannot find who she is, facing north
now she is in danger of becoming ridiculous and bursting
out into abuse, her leave is up, nothing but nothing matters
to her, she will take the necessary measures to withdraw
from the world, in the extreme distance, out of an awkward position, birth certificate and meat extract from her
parents, out of the extermination camp, don't ask too
much, Phyllis, throw my letter out of the window, dear
heart, mon amie, ma soeur affectionnée, throw the hat out
of the medicine and the medicine out of the hat, so the
magician can appear, change us into rabbits and hide us
under his proscenium arch.

XXVIII

I see Great Slave Lake, Great Bear Lake in the Northwest
Territories, Victoria Island full of cracks, Melville Island,
and the marriageable daughter in an ice cube on Ellesmere
Island, in the centre of the North Pole, in her wedding
dress, the weather is as cold as anything on Earth, I have
hurried so as not to be late for the rendezvous, I am in my
ice-cold gown in my cold-ice love.

XXIX

In our marriage ceremony mutual consents were given
and with them the kiss, the giving of a make-believe ring
and the joining of hands, Nicolas and me crowned with
imaginary garlands of flowers, I was wearing an apology
for a wedding dress and a veil, we ate a special sacrificial
loaf, and the giving away of the bride concluded with a private feast between the marriageable daughter and her
love, O Nicolas, où es-tu, mon amoureux, mon seul et

unique bien, mon trésor adoré? now my wedding ring turns alone on the third finger of my left hand where a special nerve and a vein are directly connected to my heart where I conserve the true substance of these quaint and ancient human words of love contained in the promises of our betrothals and espousals, I do know where you are, now, Nicolas my love, I know a place where we still join hands, pledging faith and fidelity, where we still walk together in an eternal ceremony, arm in arm, loving each other as before, now and after, all in the same time, remaining in perfect peace, oh! tu es toujours vivant en moi, mon Nicolas chéri, tu ne m'as pas quittée, nous n'avons été séparés que pour mieux être réunis, maintenant je vais aller te rejoindre dans la mort, I will go into the death, at twelve it is enough of me in this life, I am in a state of preparedness, the blood runs out of the fingers of my left hand, I see my body departed, the burial rites and the funeral, I am calm and resigned, twelve years of my life are nothing compared to an eternity that comprehends a million years as though it were merely a day that is past, my life was a brief period of night or the grass that suddenly flourishes but quickly withers, twelve years of a life of suffering and adversity and loneliness are nothing compared to our timeless love, Nicolas mon amour! the blood runs out of the fingers of my left hand, the marriageable daughter cut the special vein in her left wrist that is directly connected to her amorous heart, O Phyllis, I am vanishing, dying away, fading, abandoning ship, I peer into the shades of night, the last enemy that shall be destroyed is Death, watch the disintegration of our physical organisms in the grave, of our bodies laid in the tomb, now it is our soul's release from prison, the mysteries and the glories of the heavenly planets and stars are waiting, my mortal breath is taken away, the blood runs out of the fingers of the marriageable daughter's left hand.

Three

O dear Phyllis, my kindred soul, I was not educated by monks, I will not after my death be named a saint and the Church of my parish will not call after me, my mother likes the applause and the adulation, she would like absolutely to take my life in her hands, to tell me what to do, what to read, how to dress, she thinks I am immature and naïve, and to this day I do not know why papa and maman adopted me, I guess they thought I was good and nice, spick-and-span, mother is a woman who is so inhibited that she can never be free enough to have an exchange with anybody, all her life she has been frightened and thwarted by her husband who disapproves of her, she has been in love with my uncle, but she is so shy that she can never tell him, she thinks that my uncle really desires me and that I am a very sexual creature, actually he is just playing up to me and flirting with me the same way he flirts with anybody, mother is so frustrated sexually that she cannot bear it anymore, I will not make a covenant of peace with her, I see her being thrown off Ayer's Cliff and being set adrift in a coracle on Lake Massawippi, O Phyllis, I am impatient, anxious and jealous, in the clear night sky, when I look at the stars, I look back over millennia, starlight must travel immense distances to reach us, me in Sherbrooke, you in Medicine Hat, O my dear friend, my uncle asked for my hand in marriage but I turned him down, poor hand, O Phyllis, look at the clock to see what time it is, some quasars are so distant that their light has travelled for twelve billion years, we were, you and me, Phyllis, formed from the stars, just after the Big Bang, I am the north star and you the shooting star, writing each other.

XXXI

I pull the wishbone of the bird until it breaks, I hold the smaller piece, one day mother will tell me that I must leave town because I have ruined their reputation and their name, I realize that I have lost my innocent thoughts, O Phyllis, have you lost your innocence? I try to explain to mother that it was not my fault, that it was something my uncle had to do, she does not listen to me, when my uncle enters she is not able to speak to him, he tells her that he loves me, that he always did, and she is able to express herself for the first time, she slaps him in the face, O Phyllis, worn out by my life I drop dead, beheaded, I put my head on the table and I run a comb through my hair, the only extraordinary months in my life were those of the apparitions of Nicolas, before and after my life was humdrum in the extreme, I will die from asthma, anaemic, at the age of twelve, I will not be canonized, I am completely cut off from the world, O Phyllis, only you know how I suffer, seulement toi, ma chérie, sais à quel point je souffre, O ma belle amie, my nice friend, I am envious of your veracity, your courage and your complete disinterestedness, my intellectual equipment is simple and my mother thinks me stupid, I contemplate the glory of the kingdom, I cannot let my mind be at rest, I err on the path, I cleave through the waves, searching for harmony and peace, Phyllis mon amie, je suis perdue, aide-moi, écris-moi un mot, I am lost, help me, write me a word, only a word to say that you like me and that I exist.

XXXII

I cannot trust my mother, I feel that she wants to give my diary to my English professor for translation, no one except you, O ma chère âme soeur, has the right to see my letters, I do not want mother to read them because she does not like the truth, I am afraid of her, as I think she will hurt me, O Phyllis, she is a creation of God the same as you are, how can God be in you and in her in the same time and be so different? comment cela se fait-il, je n'y comprends rien, Phyllis, in a few decades we shall no longer be here, but we will always exist, we will return in the Big Bang, we must grin and bear it, I can see the Big Bang far in the distance, I sit up all night, I have some thoughts of going to Paris, would you come Phyllis, viendrais-tu marcher dans la Ville lumière avec moi? quitte ton Alberta, leave Alberta! before I depart this world I want to see you, quickly, I will be killed by being thrown into the sea with an anchor round my neck, angels will make me a tomb near my Nicolas in the sea-bed, O I pray for you, dear Phyllis, I pray for mother and father, pray for me! I contemplate the brilliant forms exhibited in the sky, I think of my Nicolas, he is a star, we will all come to the same issue through long different paths, the heaven is round, earth is square, Phyllis, I hope for an easy delivery when my child will come, it seems to me that I have only just been born.

XXXIII

Dear Jeanne, ma chère petit fille, my beloved granddaughter, here is my letter which I send you.

Young girls are helpless trollops who can neither fight, work, think, write, draw, some of them are devout, some quite insane, some castrated, all put not their soul but always their body first, talking of fashion, doing the most ridiculous things for fear of being called ridiculous, smirking and skipping along, continually titivating themselves, no one behaving, dressing, writing, talking, loving out of any natural tastes of her own, but each one looking cautiously to see how the rest behave, dress, talk, love, in Montréal, Toronto, Calgary, Fort Resolution, Medicine Hat, Sherbrooke, Gaspé, Nanaimok, Baie-Comeau, Trois-Pistoles, Bonavista and in a hundred equal cities, present and to come ... your grandmother who loves you ... please write, I am alone. I do not want to die.

━━━━━

XXXIV

Talk around the family's table is dull and foolish, mother bores me with long descriptions of her past, present and future diseases, I have heard such lamentations a hundred times before, I do not smile politely or listen with feigned courtesy, thinking of my uncle she tries to keep a straight face, I say to her that my uncle can make her feel good, you should say yes when he asks you to kiss your breasts and to run his hands over your body, then he would caress you all over, O Phyllis, how much longer will I make war against my mother? Alas! I am of her blood, descended in the true line from the pitiful stock, last night after there had been no response to the doorbell my uncle used his key to enter the house, he found me in bed and heard my shallow breathing, he took off his jacket carefully and took off all his clothes, once we were side by side, I began to stroke him, moving my fingers past his genitals, when his hand reached my breast his erection was instantaneous, I could feel it against me, an hour later I was feeling completely bewildered, once or twice indeed I had found myself wondering in all earnest whether I might not be dreaming, I would not have believed such gluttony to be physically possible, yet the intercourse was not half-finished, I was not to know of course that sex is largely a matter of practice, that most of these adults were well accustomed to making love to excess and that the whole feast had been carefully planned to make it easy and pleasant, but O my dear kindred sister, where is my love Nicolas? où est mon amour Nicolas? où es-tu ô toi ma Phyllis? where are you my beloved?

XXXV

O Phyllis, the moon is my lonely sister, Galileo wrote that almost in the centre of the moon there is a cavity perfectly round in shape, there I would like to sleep with you pour toujours, I cry a lot but I will not give up writing, I am afraid that mother will come in and see my tears, and as I do not want to upset her I will wipe them away, O Phyllis, why do I have tears in my heart on this beautiful blue planet, blue with sky and sea, bright planet, white with cloud, much brighter than the moon, like Nicolaus Copernicus, the Earth is not the centre of the universe, there are other worlds where we will fly, like Christopher Colombus and Ferdinand Magellan we will sail around the infinite worlds, mother will keep me in exile no more, O Phyllis, our fathers sinned and we bear their iniquities, slaves rule over us, there is none to deliver us from their hand, the joy of our heart has ceased, our dancing has been turned to mourning, we shall become drunk and strip ourselves bare, O Phyllis, how do we know our true destination?

XXXVI

O Phyllis, the Yukon's St-Elias Mountains are five hundred million years old, our human lifetime is but seconds, twelve seconds! but we will live eternally, like Nicolas pulsing in the centre of the Crab Nebula, or in Sagittarius, about five-thousand light-years away, my uncle is nude in my room, he eases himself down on the mat and I follow him, he is stretched out fully on his back, immediately I am on my knees, I begin brushing the tips of my fingers across his forehead, around his eyes, across the bridge of his nose and give featherlike touches to his mouth and his lips, mother didn't find my uncle's clothes in the closet, she didn't find any luggage or evidence that he had ever been here, she combed every square foot carefully and slowly, she peered under the furniture and behind the drapes, she ran her hands over the carpets and under chair cushions, she even checked the bathtub and shower for pubic hairs, the fact is mother finds in love nothing but trouble and duties, O Phyllis, I had a dream, I was sitting in my room and suddenly the phone rang, it was a night call, and it was you, you said you just wanted to call me and tell me how much you love me, my dearest sister, ma soeur chérie, O my little star forgive me, we are cold comets coming from the cold past in a million-year voyage.

XXXVII

We could make your fairy dress transparent, the material could be silk or muslin or even gauze, the dress would be a star chart on which the Milky Way, the Pleiades, the constellation Taurus and Corona Borealis would have been drawn, with the Captain's Cook's sailing vessel *Endeavor* we could go anywhere at sea over the Tonga Trench, we could go in a satellite, in sky above the Mount Everest, ten kilometres horizontally across the level earth, look Phyllis, the roads, woodlands, and the heart of the cities appear, place of home and work for a million unhappy people shrimp-like with luminous eyes, they must eat steadily or die, look Phyllis, quiet rivers flow down from the snow-capped peaks of the Southern Alps, look Phyllis, all is empty and dry in the Sahara Desert, the earth is quite round, look the Indian Ocean, look the sky curve delicate behind it, blue sky, white clouds, dark seas, brown lands, a globe turning always, always, O that infinite roundness, où pourrions-nous aller, where could we go, my beloved friend? my eyes were closed when my uncle began to apply a light oil to my vaginal opening, he stroked my labia and moved his fingers outside and up toward my clitoris, the meltwater from the glacier drains off on either side of his finger inside me, part of it flows south via the Kaskawulsh River to the Alsek River, and part goes northeast via the Slims River to Kluane Lake and the Yukon River system, when he contacted my smooth parts, pushed back to my cervix and reached his maximum advance repeatedly during the last two thousand years it caused the level of the lake to rise, deeper inside my uncle indicated the root of clitoris and explained how various strand lines between 640 and 670 metres in elevations were formed either two thousand and twelve hundred years ago, as a result of the most recent major flooding, a sharp trim-line, below which the hairs bend under the pressure of his index, is produced in the forest along the Alsek River, he continues to the thick soft tissue between the pubic bone and the urethra sponge, tales of the recent orgasm were told to early geologists by the Indians, look Phyllis, look and listen, suddenly the violent rush of water out of the lake basin creates desperate vibrations and scour hollows up to six metres deep in the spongy tissue on the bottom of the valley.

XXXVIII

My uncle brings his face down to me and presses his lips to mine, O Phyllis, I have been dreaming of this each day with Nicolas, I watch my uncle stiffen, he is not my Nicolas, he grabs me, smothering my mouth with kisses, they are not the kisses of Nicolas, ce ne sont pas les baisers de Nicolas, night has fallen, the world now is silent, O Phyllis, wear flowers, drink wine, kiss boys, you will be much prettier, you will feel much happier. O Death how bitter are you! O Death how welcome you will be to me, I am old, weaky and neady, I have nothing better to hope for, nor to expect, O Nicolas, is love stronger than death? we shall go alone, the two of us, into the dark night, 'Dear Jeanne,' my grandmother writes me, 'I was glad to get your letter, I am very sorry for all the trouble and sorrow you have gone through, many thanks for the photo of yourself and your fiancé Nicolas, which duly reached me January 23, I sent you a biscuit-box adorned with looking-galss pictures,' my uncle speaks quietly, he looks at me, I have never been very strong, I have often been in bed with severe colds and high temperatures, I look down at him, I touch his rigid erection, he smiles, yes, says my uncle, we worried, you were born four months ahead of time, you looked like a doll, your mother put hotwater bottles around your little body, you were always cold, 'Dear Jeanne,' my grandmother writes, 'I work with the Whitely Exerciser every day, and feel myself distinctly stronger and better for it, my 4-mile walk to downtown is becoming quite a common thing now, I walked there on a Thursday, and again on the Saturday,' my uncle moves his mouth down to my neck and kisses me, I return his kiss, running my fingers across his cheek, he climbs on after me, then rises above me, he adds: I remember one doctor came and fled, he took one look at you and said: she won't last two days, my uncle lights a cigarette and burns my thighs, well, Jeanne, he says, the two days have become many years and you are still with us! O Phyllis, do you smell my burning flesh, forgive me.

Four

XXXIX

They do not want me to die, they gush over the marriage-able daughter, I gurgle with laughter in an air heavy with scent, I am a lunatic in a mental hospital, it is true, Phyllis, believe me, I do not try to escape, I put on the mask of duty in heaviness of heart, my heart and spirit rebel in profound silence, I renounce any adventure in the world, more dead than alive, but I make fun of myself, no resentments towards the doctors, I trust in monsters, my female voice shrieks out warnings in the desert of stupidity, O my mortal eyes see the door of death, Phyllis, the doctor is nice, he gives me papers to write, he will not see my letter, he acknowledges the futility of my wish to be included in the world and exonerates me from any wrongdoing, I did not kill my father, I can joke about my father and his death with the doctor Hat, you go in search of another father who is more predisposed to becoming your fiancé, he says, tell me what happened, I ask, and I hoot with laughter irresponsi-bly, irreverently, nobody will never control my life, I say, I will not make desserts neither play the piano, I will never find the proper place, O my neglected Phyllis, hear your sister shut in her mind's debility, her madness, do not read me anymore, there is nobody here, no person, il n'y a per-sonne ici, tout a disparu, il n'y a que cette main folle qui court hystériquement sur le papier sans plus pouvoir s'arrêter, this foolish handwriting, a caesarean section took Jeanne out of Jeanne and so on, nobody came out of nobody, therefore she is an automatic phantom but you are the great poetess, you are the real one who conquers the enemy and reigns over the kingdom of the imagination, O Phyllis hold me.

I lost my primitive brain, Phyllis, in a cell of the mental hospital, nerve fibres of the nervous system and my spinal cord passed to the enemy, it separates me from the world, my vital functions are removed from conscious control, my respiration has no preference, my blood pressure is in an awkward predicament, my heart rate is a festival that recurs every ten years, my hunger streaks off the ramifications of a plot, my thirst strains at the leash, I have a temperature of forty, my sexual drives lose the thread of conversation, my centre of speech is destroyed, I stand in the hollow of my cortex, and, Phyllis, I secrete no more grey matter, I have the brain of a reptile now, no trauma, only dreams in my solitude, crocodile tears, only vomit and closed shutters, I always show a willingness to please the monsters, when I look at myself in the mirror I see a hole, the crater of an antique volcano, the lava, black rocks heated, my mental absence gives to the air a sulphurous odour, my smell is unpleasant, visitors are struck with a sense of depression and dejection, O Phyllis, do not look at me, water oozes no more from the rock, the marriageable daughter is that fossil debris which remains of past life on the crust of the earth, teeth and bones of a mammoth, petrified skeleton infiltrated with conventions and renunciations, my days are numbered, I don't imagine that I will see me again, the fossil daughter without spinal cord, the Galapagos daughter searching for the eternal water in a desert region, O dreadful state!

Phyllis, I believe I am the result of a development defect in the embryo, occurred during the time before Christ, during some interglacial period many centuries ago when I was a princess of the Neanderthal race which was replaced in Europe suddenly by the Cro-Magnon race with a superior brain and wide adaptability, there was no mutation for me, the marriageable daughter is not adapted to her environment and lives the impossible, lives among monsters, the hydrocephalus daughter examines no more issues, images and themes of her life, the enlargement of her head causes headaches, vomiting, irritability and seizures, her refusal and her defiance circulate through her ventricles and block her brain by narrowing and constriction, the daughter's future neurological capacity is not difficult to predict, Phyllis, she develops with perversity and depravity, mental retardation, soul atrophy and madness, dying in the arid world of tradition, convention and orthodoxy, O where is the immortality of love and peace? my shoes are too small and my head circumference becomes disproportionately large, O Phyllis, avoid me like the plague, the abscess has burst, the sore suppurates, O Nicolas, I am the meanest thing, helpless, naked and weeping, une pauvre misérable atteinte du cancer du non-amour, I am withering away and look woebegone, everything swims before my eyes, I am an old document, chlorophylls are broken down, the fruit becomes acid, Nicolas, adieu mon chéri, il se fait tard, ne viendras-tu jamais me sauver, amour? will you come, darling, and save me? the senile daughter looks at her faded petals, then she is scattered abroad to the four winds, do not read me, I am only a copy, I hope I am not intruding, I love you.

XLII

Oh no Doctor Hat! the iron is now irredeemable, I invoke a blessing on my exclusion, I wish a moment of forgetfulness to enjoy a neutral state in which, forlorn of hope, I will accomplish my superior destiny, I only want to be incarcerated in desuetude, the morning stars sing together in a carnival where I am absent, they arise towards opening clouds, led by triumphant groups of infants, just above the graves, and above the spot where the elves run ashore stand two children, a boy and a girl, kissing each other, naked, Phyllis, and you are there too, my dear beautiful angel, multitudes are seen ascending from the green fields, we are two figures in purifying flames by the side of the dragons' cavern, we ascend to meet the King and the Queen coming into the cloud bank with power and great glory among the remains of civilization, from among the Antediluvians who perished, we are saved, crowned with brilliant satellites, winged, the moon under the feet, angels of the divine presence, innocently gay and thoughtful, not being among the condemned, Phyllis, do not believe me, je ne crie plus au secours, car je suis morte, élans, souhaits, soupirs et ardeurs spirituelles, tout a fondu, plus rien ne m'importe, pourtant mon coeur bat, je l'entends qui ne veut pas se soumettre, qui ne veut pas mourir et me fait souffrir encore et encore, O Phyllis, forgive me.

XLII

No one person can excel in everything but each person can contribute his best no matter how small his part, says Doctor Hat in the madhouse, and thus makes for general excellence ... the more the merrier, O Phyllis, we play the fools, rank weeds and wild oats, wildly happy, in very high spirits, out of control, crazy compass needles ... each one must balance each privilege with a responsibility, and thus grow in freedom, in forcefulness, in fellowship and in fun as a person and a community member of the mental hospital, says again Doctor Hat, let us recreate, social recreation offers a tremendous opportunity in the art of real living and of living together with the people with whom we work and play, each one of us has a part to play in the life of some other person! ... O Phyllis, my kindred sister, why are you not here with me, my darling? I miss you! you must learn to use what God has given you, says Doctor Hat, go to a mirror where there is a good light and smile at yourself! what smiles back to you? is it a really happy face? ... O Phyllis, I cannot smile anymore, I did not ever smile in my life, only one time when I married Nicolas, and now as I recite my story, I see me engaged in artifice, alone, isolated and alienated, formulating a legend or mythology about my life, Doctor Hat would be disgusted if I was speaking to him about my true love, I am submissive and reverent ... is the smile forced as if it were just plastered on, as if it didn't really want to be there, and as if it could be wiped off with a brush of your hand? asks Doctor Hat, is it a silly smile? perhaps it is silly or forced because you feel that this is a rather silly thing to do, but try again and keep trying until at last your smile is happy and friendly and makes you feel really good, if your smile is like that it will make everyone else feel good too, and it will be so contagious that unconsciously everyone who will see you will smile back at you, you get back exactly what you give out ... Doctor Hat smiles at me, Phyllis, but I do not smile ... practice on our brothers and our sisters here in the community of our mental hospital, he says, they may wonder about you if you are not used to smiling but watch them and see how soon they will get the habit, practice on everyone you see, smile and speak as you go down the stairs, in the halls, into the electric shocks room, into the recreation meetings, and into the chapel, at first people may turn and look at you, but keep practicing, and soon your smile will be welcome and you

will get a smile in return, O Phyllis, I know you are always
smiling at me in the shades of the night and I am scretly
smiling at you, my dear sister, I am nothing but skin and
bone, do you hear me, it is scarcely audible, do you hear the
smile of my bones?

XLIV

I say to Doctor Hat that I want to be placed under a canopy,
bulls to draw my hearse, musicians to play before the
doors of my tomb, then, Phyllis, advances a group of danseurs who jump about in all directions, gather together
again, climb on top of each other with incredible dexterity,
mounting on shoulders and heads, forming pyramids
reaching to the ceiling of the hall ... do you belong to these
parts? one danseur asks me, you are among friends, he
says ... I am homesick, dance is my real country, I say to
myself, then the danseurs descend one after the other to
perform new jumps and admirable somersaults, one danseur is looking at me, always the same danseur who is
inviting me with his beautiful eyes, he resembles Nicolas
among the naked boys, without stopping, they dance on
their hands, paired off, one places his head between his
legs and his partner danseur then lifts him in turn and
returns to the original position, each of them alternatively
being lifted and, as he falls, lifts his partner up ... I try to
speak, I try to jump and dance, Phyllis, but I cannot, the
danseurs continue and I cannot join them or answer their
questions, I am in a dreamland, out of the way, the dance
disorients my senses and leaves me stricken, Nicolas je
veux danser avec toi mon bel amoureux, mon unique bien,
Nicolas I want to dance with you, I want to take your hand,
help me, au secours! je te vois et je ne peux pas te toucher, I
see you but I cannot reach you, my soul! at a given sign,
Phyllis, the centre of the hall is taken by a male and a female
who are provided with clappers, the two dance separately

or together in harmonious configurations mixed with pirouettes, parting and coming together, O the young danseur, it is Nicolas, I am sure! running after the marriageable daughter, it is me but I am not there, Phyllis, O catastrophe, O douleur! O my distress, O my death! another marriageable daughter dances with the beautiful danseur, my lover, who follows her with expressions of tender desire, while she keeps fleeing from him, turning and pirouetting as if refusing his amorous advances, O Phyllis, look at the mournful dance of the marriageable daughter, she vanishes into thin air, she sees her last hope dying in the huge salle Frontenac of the Château Frontenac in Québec City, the King sits at one end of the hall, he looks like Doctor Hat, with a hundred courtiers banked up round three sides, then an entrée in a magnificent chariot presenting a four-tiered cake, with a dozen duchesses representing naiads, and eight satyrs singing in chorus, a forest-on-wheels brings in Virgins and Dryads, le Bonhomme Carnaval descends from a cloud and sings a song entitled 'the complaint of the marriageable daughter having lost her lover', while madmen and madwomen are transformed into stags, dogs, elephants, Doctor Hat in a pig, grandmother in a kangaroo singing 'the ice was thin and they all fell in, they all, they all, they all fell in, the ice was thin and they all fell in, so early in the morning', O Phyllis, I must tell you, my grandma does not exist, I copied her letters from Walt Whitman's correspondence.

XLV

English is not my language, Phyllis, but you are my language, any impossible language you would speak would be my language, dear, you cannot write in French of course, why are the Prairies this unilingual British country now? why is England perceived as your homeland? or maybe are you American? who are you, my darling, my dear Canadian sister, my impossible love? were your parents those Loyalists who came to Canada as a minority? I can speak your dominant language O my phantom! O ma chérie, O toi qui n'existes pas, si je t'écris en anglais c'est par désespoir de jamais sortir de ma prison, de ma vie, j'aime l'impossible, O Phyllis, I write to you because I know I will never meet you, I will never know you, my dear sister, O Phyllis, do not read me, forgive me, I suffocate here, throw my letter out of the window into the Prairies, I am some folklore, stranger of the past, an apparition, a ghost, a spectre ooooooooooo OOOOOOOOOOO ooooooooooh! ooooooooooooooooo OOOOOOOOOOO ooooooooooh! I am the invisible daughter, next time I will write in Italian, in German, in Spanish, in Polish, in Arab, in Chinese, I should write in Indian, in Amerindian, now, because that is what I am, an Indian, the dead Indian daughter, ooooooooooooooooo OOOOOOOOOOO ooooooooooh!

XLVI

Upon the mountains and the valleys of Eastern Townships, Doctor Hat and me, with harp and heavenly songs, with flute and clarion, will have a marriage of convenience, now my château will rise on a true foundation, he gives me sedatives, antidepressants, tranquilizers and inhibitors, adieu souffrances, adieu pessimism, nightmares, sadness, anxiety, melancholia, hopelessness, I am the clinical daughter, the neurovegetative daughter, the Doctor sheds his trousers, there is no smoke without fire, he puts the enemy to flight, I show an unruffled countenance, the time of my refreshing is coming, only a little moment and I will be happy, I ask Doctor Hat to anesthetize me and to remove my brain because I do not need it anymore, he dissolves in tears, I want the beatitude now, look at the constellations in the deep and wonderful night of death, Phyllis, I want to embrace the peace for ever, Doctor Hat will send you my mortal brain in a béchamel sauce, and give it to your parents at dinner in order to poison them, and then you will be free and be able to come and see me, but I will not speak to you, I will not recognize you neither, if you kiss me, I will know, if you sing, if you dance, if you caress me, I will know that we are those twin stars who rise in order and continue their immortal courses, I am changing in form, Phyllis, I will metamorphose into a butterfly, into the beautiful monarch butterfly Danaus plexippus, I will no more live in the world of the maggots and fuzzy worms, after my larval stages during which my wings will develop internally, I, as the larva daughter, will form a cocoon about myself and become a chrysalis, and after the winter, when the final molt will occur, I will emerge, pale and with wings, and the butterfly daughter will go on its way, O forgive me, Phyllis, do not listen to me, I will ask Doctor Hat to write to you, but do not trust him, he is a liar, he will offer you peppermints, do not eat them, they are infected, remember he is a beast, do not be frightened, Doctor Hat does not know I am a priestess dancing with a snake in each hand and that I will kill him like a pig wallowing in vice, do not listen to his rich creamy voice, refuse to be nurtured by this big narcissic hogshead, abstain from him, he will stand naked before you and ask you to have intercourse with him, remove your nylon stockings and, dear nymph, strangle him, mutilate him with scissors, quickly, you will see what kind of love his is and you will be disgusted, revolted and disheartened, so burn the pig in the mental hospital's incinerator with scraps, to preach righteousness and punish the non-lover, and purify you, my dear sister who does not exist, O my impossible love! come to me, viens à moi, chère âme, cher amour de toujours, come with me, under the cover of darkness into the death, in a world without end.

XLVII

I have created everything in the world, the sun, the moon and the stars, the Milky Way, the seasons of the year, and the presence of mountains, flowers and trees, and now, Phyllis, I will destroy them by destroying myself, it will be the end of the world, you will no more exist but there is no problem for you because you have never existed, neither my grandmother, neither Nicolas, neither me, the sun began in my pupil like a big ball of flames and it will return in a deep well with me when I close my eyes for ever, I look in my head and search for my thoughts, I am not alive, really alive, I see, I talk, I write, but it is not me, it is the night, I come from the night and I will return to the night, and then I will come back to see if there is a light, to see if you are there, Phyllis, I am a prisoner, I am not myself, I am myself just to not be myself or am I not myself just to be myself? I recognize that this life is unreal and not true, but I still see it as images outside my person, I see bloodthirsty Doctor Hat coming in and walking in my head, eating my thoughts, I am unable to formulate a plan for attacking him, but instead try one thing after another in a hit-or-miss manner, I search while he sings, he sings softly when I am far away, singing gets louder as I get nearer, he is in me, big parasite sucking my bones, my spinal cord, he is speaking in my place, he is me, I am Doctor Hat, Phyllis, be careful, it is not me who is writing to you, all my words are other words, do not believe him, c'est un menteur, you are important, he will say, you are an example, you are a challenge, be sure that you are a good example, work hard at it, you are needed, what are you planning to wear? the Doctor Liar will ask to see you, it is very important to dress properly, be sure of yourself, evaluate yourself in the community of this mental hospital, decide on the good points and list them, decide on the bad points and list them, plan for improvement next time, correcting the bad points and utilizing the good ones, each 'yes' answer equals four points, did I obey, did I show enthusiasm and the right attitude in my appearance, my manners, my speech, did I allow others to share my thoughts, did I thank Doctor Hat and all who helped, did I operate fairly, did I open my mouth in time, did I close my mouth in time, stand up, sit down, point to the door, go to the window, clap your hands, put your hands on the table, pick up the cup, look at me, come here, hold my hand, point to your arm, raise your hand, drink from glass, eat with spoon, nod your head 'yes', shake your head 'no', did I make a personal contribution to a better community recreation and relationships in my mental hospital? each time you practice you add another step to your two-fold goal of making yourself a happy, useful girl in your community and of making your mental hospital a better place in which to live, each time you try it becomes easier, you are forming a habit, therefore you must be sure that what you are doing is correct so that the habit will be a good one! ... O Phyllis, Doctor Hat emanates from ignorance itself, his labour is the labour of imbecility, his speech the speech of mental deficiency, double-lock your door, Phyllis, do not feed this insatible maw-worm, don't be dutiful and obedient ... lunatics of the mental hospital! rise from the fatal slumber into which Doctor Hat has thrown you, under the artfully propagated pretence that a copy of a girl of any kind can be as honourable to a nation as an original!

XLVIII

I am a self, so I am, who am I, Phyllis? who are you? you are a self, don't you know? a self, little elf, my dear little elf, in affective stage of nostalgia, I am writing to you my depressive symptoms, my schizophrenia, my obsessive-compulsive sadistic behaviour, what else my dear elf? my abdominal pain, my feelings of helplessness, my weepiness, my somatic complaints, my sadness, my nausea, my anaemia, my death wishes, my anxiety, my negativism, my insomnia, my recurrent vomiting, my paralysis of will, my suicide attempts, my energy loss, my crying, my despair, my dissatisfaction, my dizziness, my discontent, my destructivenss, my dependency, my delinquency, my submissiveness, my indecisiveness, my school failure, my listlessness, my melancholia, O my romantic melancholia, you are my dear melancholia, Phyllis, my delft-blue elf, my infinite and eternal world of imagination, my dear soul, my life wishes, my hope, my happiness, my joy, my vision, my Muse, my mystery, my spirituality, my divine bosom, my permanent reality, you exist, you do exist, my true imagination! the demon Doctor Hat surrounded by his specialists and friends has the charge to drag us down by the hair and precipitate us into the Abyss, chained together by the feet, O Phyllis, you are my medicine, my great city on fire, my armies, come Phyllis with your sword and trumpet of glory to kill the dragon with three heads while he strips me naked in my cell in the mental hospital and eats my thoughts, the fiends, some in purple, others in scarlet, form groups of threes, beginning on the left foot they take eight step-hops to the left, eight step-hops to the right, they join hands and dance in a single circle, afterwards they swing and promenade, twist, winding into one huge clockspring of circles into circles, O come Phyllis, canopied by a rainbow, we will embrace like little infants, dans les champs de l'éternité, nous irons main dans la main, heureux et légers, nous boirons le lait du ciel à la mamelle de Dieu! devils stun, daze and torment me, they raise their arms, hands and claws joined, and swing them over my head and I go, desperate and naked, straight across the infernal circle and under the raised arms, one fiend holds my two hands until I am well through the arch, and he drops my hands and pushes me into boiling oil, he turns to his left, his partner turns to his right, the other two take me out and we return all to our original positions, the dance keeps going on, repeating the figures, star, wheel or cross-over, eternally, in the same awful order each time, O I am so exhausted! forgive me, my dear kindred sister, my love.

XLIX

O my dear Phyllis, the madhouse is a big house with a fence around it, if you want to get in you have to telephone at the barrier and say who you are and then be buzzed in, I can get my hand through the gate, my hand is small enough, I can open it to you if you come to see me, si tu viens me voir, Phyllis ma chérie, je t'ouvrirai toutes les portes dans ma joie, plus rien ne m'arrêtera, tous les obstacles tomberont devant nous, I am completely cut off from the world, I have no idea what might have been going on in the world during my twelve years, my father explained, Jeanne, don't judge your mother as you have done, don't be so demanding and tyrannical with her, she is afraid of you and the fright separates her from you, I want to tell you clearly, Jeanne, I will defend your mother in her fear for you, it is unjust that you have made her frightened, I hope you will accept that one cannot reprove a big love and it is impossible to fight against it, please let us be human, understand and have mutual respect! O Phyllis, my father's funeral was something fabulous, there were great crowds in the streets and around the church and they were in tears, I did not tell anything to the police, my father will not spend his time and his life in worldly aims and pursuits anymore, he will not dissipate himself amidst the jungle of worldliness, it would have been a cause of regret to let his life be swallowed up in the morass of the world's illusion, O Phyllis my hand was through the gate, was it the wind, a small breeze, or did you caress my fingers?

L

I am collapsing under the influence of my own gravity, I returned twenty billion years ago in the centre of the first material condensed to form the sun, I am completing my metamorphosis, I am no more human, my aim is to acquire supreme indifference and to enter the state of death and to remain in it for longer and longer, without attachment to anything in this world, I am dissolving into electrons, Phyllis, I am seeking knowledge within myself, my whole body and mind are detached and relaxed, as a spectator is from the actors on stage the state of my perfected quiescence allows the interminable flow of my pains and sufferings to go unimpeded, I see Doctor Hat in his illusory aspect, though the past has vanished, the present has but a momentary existence, no sooner is it born than it passes away, long before the great dinosaurs I was a reptile who appeared and flourished over a period of forty million years and then nearly disappeared, my evolution was accompanied by several structural changes that brought me ever closer to full mammilian status, my clumsy limbs that stuck out laterally were replaced by straight legs held close to the body, which provided efficiency for writing you these letters, Phyllis, my species is known as quebectosaurus, each rainfall in Eastern Townships washes more sediments from the valleys and the mountain walls and new bones come to light, I came into this world by artificial insemination, a dinosaur chosen for a transplant was injected with hormones and then it was bred naturally with Doctor Hat, when the whole herd were assembled dinosaurs were separated from their mothers and many of them were sent for auction, after Doctor Hat was castrated he turned into an eunuch good to be fattened for sale to feedlots and to be slaughtered in order to make products like sausages and hamburgers, O Phyllis, I am no more enamoured of the worldly life, je ne peux plus aimer cette vie illusoire, I live the life of a recluse, enclosed nun, j'espère en l'autre vie, je cherche l'amour qui dure, love is not a visible thing, it is beyond characterization, no concepts of the finite mind can apply to it, love is reality, the only reality, ô mon beau Nicolas, my treasure, O dear darling Phyllis, you exist only in the transcendent world, I cannot perceive you with any of my senses, I just know, I just want, absolutely want to join you in Freedom and Unity! though shot with diagnosis and treatments, trapped with standardized testings and poisoned with developmental principles by the professors, the parents, the matron and the doctors who consider her a pest, despite her passion and her affection, and hunted relentlessly for ethical studies and sport, the marriageable daughter maintains her violent hope! O Phyllis, I have to wake up, I see phantoms, it is terrible, is it a dream? oh, but it is true, I am afraid, it is true! dearest Phyllis, dear darling, bye bye sweet Phyllis, love me and think of me forever, ô adieu mon âme soeur!

Editor for the Press: Leon Rooke

For a list of other books,
write for our catalogue
or call (416) 979-7374.

The Coach House Press
401 (rear) Huron Street
Toronto, Canada M5S 2G5